LITTLE RED RIDING HOOD

LITTLE RED RIDING HOOD

BY THE BROTHERS GRIMM

RETOLD AND ILLUSTRATED BY
TRINA SCHART HYMAN

HOLIDAY HOUSE
· NEW YORK ·

FOR MIMI

Library of Congress Cataloging in Publication Data

Hyman, Trina Schart.
Little Red Riding Hood.

Summary: On her way to deliver a basket
of food to her sick grandmother, Elisabeth
encounters a sly wolf.
[1. Fairy tales.   2. Folklore—Germany]
I. Grimm, Jacob, 1785–1863. Rotkäppchen.
II. Little Red Riding Hood. English.
PZ8.H994Li   1983   398.2′1′0943   [E]   82-7700
AACR2
ISBN 0-8234-0470-6
ISBN 0-8234-0653-9 (pbk.)

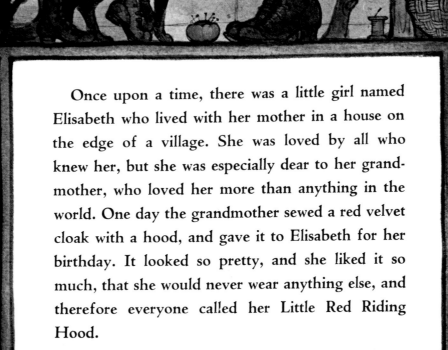

Once upon a time, there was a little girl named Elisabeth who lived with her mother in a house on the edge of a village. She was loved by all who knew her, but she was especially dear to her grandmother, who loved her more than anything in the world. One day the grandmother sewed a red velvet cloak with a hood, and gave it to Elisabeth for her birthday. It looked so pretty, and she liked it so much, that she would never wear anything else, and therefore everyone called her Little Red Riding Hood.

Early one morning her mother said to her, "Come here, Red Riding Hood, and listen to me. I want you to take this loaf of fresh bread, some of this sweet butter, and a bottle of wine to your grandmother. She is sick in bed, and they will do her a world of good. Go right away, before the sun gets too hot. Promise me that you won't daydream and stray off the path, and don't run, or you will fall down and break the bottle, and then there will be no wine for Grandmother. And when you get there, please don't forget your manners! Say 'Good morning,' 'Please,' and 'Thank you' nicely, without staring 'round about you or sucking your finger. Don't stay too long, or else you will tire Grandmother. And when you have had a nice visit, come straight home."

"Yes, Mama," said Little Red Riding Hood. "I promise. I will do just as you tell me."

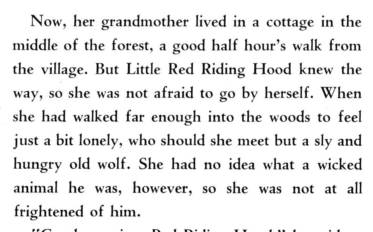

Now, her grandmother lived in a cottage in the middle of the forest, a good half hour's walk from the village. But Little Red Riding Hood knew the way, so she was not afraid to go by herself. When she had walked far enough into the woods to feel just a bit lonely, who should she meet but a sly and hungry old wolf. She had no idea what a wicked animal he was, however, so she was not at all frightened of him.

"Good morning, Red Riding Hood," he said.

"Good morning, Wolf," she answered politely.

"Where are you off to so early in the day, my dear?" he asked.

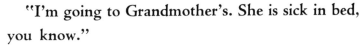

"I'm going to Grandmother's. She is sick in bed, you know."

"Is that so?" he murmured. "And what have you got in your basket?"

"A loaf of bread, some sweet butter, and a bottle of wine. Mama and I baked yesterday, so I'm taking a loaf to Grandmother. It will do her a world of good."

"Now, isn't that nice. And where does your grandmother live, Little Red Riding Hood?"

"Oh, it's a good fifteen minutes farther into the wood. Her house is the one by those three big oak trees, right next to the blackberry hedge, and there's a stream running by her garden. Surely you know the place," said Little Red Riding Hood.

The wolf thought to himself, "Aha! This tender little creature will be a plump morsel! A good dessert after the old woman. I must be clever about this, so that I can make a good meal out of the two of them!"

He walked along with Little Red Riding Hood for a while, making polite conversation. Then he said, "Just look at those beautiful wildflowers, Red Riding Hood! They are a sight even for my tired, old eyes. For goodness' sake, why don't you relax a bit, look at the world, and see how lovely it is? Why, I don't believe you even hear the birds sing, or enjoy the sunshine! You are just as solemn and well behaved as if you were going to school. Everything else is so gay and happy out here in the forest."

Then Little Red Riding Hood looked away from the path, and when she saw the sunlight dancing through the trees, and the wild flowers and butterflies scattered throughout the ferns, she thought, "I'm sure that Grandmother would feel happier if I took her a bunch of flowers. They are a sight for tired, old eyes, I know. And it is still quite early in the day. I'll have plenty of time to pick them."

So she excused herself, said good-bye to the wolf, and wandered off among the trees to pick flowers. Each time she picked one, she always saw another, even prettier one farther away. And so she left the path, and went deeper and deeper into the forest.

Meanwhile, the wicked wolf went straight off to the grandmother's cottage, and knocked softly at the door.

"Who's there?" called the grandmother from
her bed.

"It's me, Little Red Riding Hood!" said the wolf
in a tiny voice. "I've brought you a loaf of bread,
some sweet butter, and a bottle of wine. Let me in!"

"You'll have to lift the latch and let yourself in,
dear," the grandmother called out. "I'm feeling too
weak to get out of bed."

So the wolf lifted the latch and opened the door.
He ran straight to the bed, and without even saying
a good-morning, he ate up the poor old grandmother
in one gulp. Then he put on a clean nightgown
and shawl that were lying on a chair by the bedside,
got into the bed, and pulled the bed-curtains closer
together.

In the meantime, Little Red Riding Hood wandered here and there picking flowers until she had such an armful she could barely hold them all. Then she suddenly remembered her grandmother and the promise she had made to her mother. So she found her way back to the path, and walked straight to the cottage.

When she got there, she was amazed to find the door open, and she tiptoed in. She felt quite frightened, but she didn't know why. "What's wrong?" she thought. "I always like coming to Grandmother's so much. Why should I feel so afraid? Can it be because she is sick?"

"Good morning, Grandmother," she called. But there was no answer. Then she went quietly into the bedroom and pulled the bed-curtains back. There lay her grandmother. But she had drawn her shawl down over her face, and she looked very odd. Red Riding Hood couldn't help but stare.

"Grandmother! What big, hairy ears you have grown!" she said.

"The better to hear you with, my dear."

"Oh, Grandmother! Your eyes are so shiny!"

"The better to see you with, my dear."

"Your hands look so strange, Grandmother!"

"The better to catch you and hug you with, my dear."

"Please, Grandmother, why do you have such big, sharp teeth?"

"Those are to eat you up with, my dear!"

As the wolf said this, he sprang out of bed and ate up poor Little Red Riding Hood! Then, having finished his first good meal in many weeks, that wicked wolf went back to bed, pulled the covers up, and soon was snoring as loudly as you can imagine.

Not long after that, a huntsman from the village happened to be passing by the grandmother's cottage. "By jiminy," he thought. "The old lady is snoring much too loudly! Maybe I should stop in and see if there is anything the matter with her." So he went right into the house and up to the bed, where he saw the wolf fast asleep in the grandmother's nightgown and shawl, with a fat stomach full to bursting.

Right away, the huntsman guessed what had happened.

"So, here you are, you old sinner," the huntsman said. "I've been looking for you all these years, and now this is where I find you."

He raised his gun to shoot, but then he wondered if the wicked old wolf might have swallowed the grandmother whole, and if perhaps there was a chance she still might be saved. So he took out his knife and quickly killed the wolf while he lay sleeping. Then he carefully cut open the wolf's stomach.

At the first cut, he saw the red velvet cloak, and after a few more slashes a little girl jumped out and cried, "Oh, thank you! I was very frightened! It was so dark inside the wolf!" Next the grandmother climbed out, alive but hardly able to breathe from fright and exhaustion. They thanked the huntsman with all their hearts, and he was so glad to see them both alive and well that he hugged Little Red Riding Hood and shook the grandmother's hand over and over again.

They were all quite happy. The huntsman skinned the wolf and took the pelt home to nail on his door. Little Red Riding Hood and her grandmother sat down together to eat the fresh bread and sweet butter. The grandmother drank some of the wine, and Red Riding Hood had a cup of blackberry tea. After a while, the grandmother felt quite strong and healthy, and began to clean up the mess that the wolf had left in the cottage.

As Little Red Riding Hood walked home through the woods, she thought to herself, "I will never wander off the forest path again, as long as I live. I should have kept my promise to my mother." She was comforted, though, that she had at least minded her manners, and had always said "Good morning," "Please," and "Thank you."

DATE DUE

AUG - 1 2003	JUN 3 0 2005
AUG 2 0 2003	JUL 2 0 2005
SEP 2 4 2003	AUG 1 8 2005
OCT 2 5 2003	OCT 2 5 2005
FEB 1 0 2004	NOV 1 7 2005
	MAR 2 7 2006
MAR 2 4 2004	APR 0 5 2006
APR 1 8 2004	
JUL 2 0 2004	
SEP 2 4 2004	
NOV 2 3 2004	
DEC 2 3 2004	
MMAR 2 1 2005	
APR 2 2 2005	
JUN 2 1 2005	